HELLO, BUNNIES!

R MY FABULOUS
NEIGHBOURS
USI AND DAVID

THE NEW NEIGHBOURS

BY
SARAH McINTYRE

THE NEW NEIGHBOURS
is a DAVID FICKLING BOOK
t published in Great Britain in 2018
by David Fickling Books,
31 Beaumont Street,
Oxford, OX1 2NP

www.davidficklingbooks.com

Text and illustrations
© Sarah McIntyre, 2018

1 3 5 7 9 10 8 6 4 2

ght of Sarah McIntyre to be identified
e author and illustrator of this work
een asserted in accordance with the
right, Designs and Patents Act 1988.

NING: This book may contain traces
of rabbit poo

Hardback: 978 1 910200 58 2
Paperback: 978 1 910989 01 2

pers used by David Fickling Books
are from well-managed forests
and other responsible sources.

MIX
Paper from
responsible sources
FSC® C104723
www.fsc.org

DAVID FICKLING BOOKS
Reg. No. 8340307

CIP catalogue record for this book
available from the British Library.

Printed and bound in China
by Toppan Leefung

David Fickling Books

CLOVIS
OSCAR
PIPER
JAKE
ROSIE

High on the roof, above the city, Mr Pigeon had the latest news.

"You've got RATS in your flats!" he burbled with glee. "They moved in today on the ground floor."

"RATS!" squealed the bunnies.
"RATS!
RATS!
RATS!
YIPPEE!!"

The bunnies were so
excited that they

BOUNCED

down

the

stairs

to tell their

big sister,

Lettuce.

"Guess what!" shouted Piper.
"We have RATS in our flats!"

Lettuce said, "Hmm . . . RATS!
I've never lived with RATS before . . .

. . . We should go and say hi.

Let's see if Vern wants to come."

All the bunnies

HOPPED

down
the
stairs.

"Hi, Vern!" said Lettuce. "Some rats have just moved in downstairs. Do you want to come and say hello?"

"RATS?" mused Vern. "I don't think rats are very tidy neighbours. We need to make sure they keep the place clean. Let's gather everyone in the building and figure out what to do."

The rabbits and Vern HOPPED and TROTTED downstairs to talk to the pigs.

RRRR

WHOOSH

"Walter! Matilda!" said Vern. "We have **RATS** in our flats! We need to make sure these **RATS** know our rules about keeping this building spick-and-span."

"**RATS**?" grunted Walter. "Oh, no!"

Matilda huffed. "Heavens! Rats are messy *and* they SMELL BAD, too. This is AWFUL news! I bet I know what the polar bears are going to say."

Everyone

HOPPED

and

TROTTED

and TOTTERED

downstairs . . .

"Lars! Astrid! You're not going to like this!" said Matilda.
"Smelly, messy RATS just moved in downstairs!"
"WHAT?" said Astrid. "Rats are smelly and messy . . .
and they like to steal food!"

WHAT!?

BURP

EW!

Lars looked worried. "What will we eat if they steal all our food? We must tell the yaks this TERRIBLE NEWS!"

WOULD THEY STEAL MY TEDDY, TOO?

Everyone

HOPPED

and TROTTED

and TOTTERED

and PADDED

downstairs . . .

"Norbu! Pemba! We're in trouble!" said Lars. "BIG TROUBLE! Dirty, stinking, thieving RATS are now living downstairs. And I've heard that rats love to chew through walls! The WHOLE BUILDING might fall down!"

Norbu and Pemba gasped in horror.

Pemba's voice trembled. "We must DO something!"

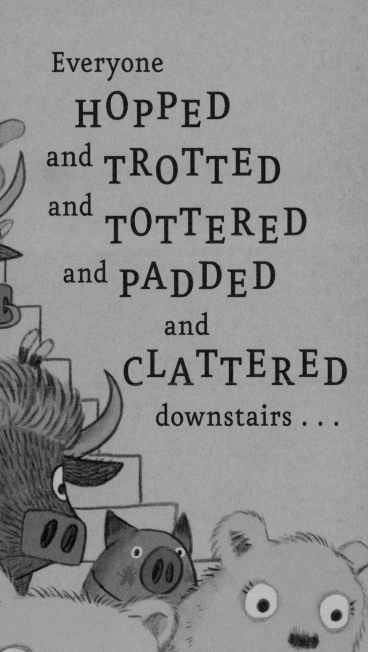

Everyone
HOPPED
and **TROTTED**
and **TOTTERED**
and **PADDED**
and
CLATTERED
downstairs . . .

"RATS!
BIG, DIRTY,
SMELLY, THIEVING,
DANGEROUS RATS
have moved in downstairs and they are going to
make the whole building collapse and bury us
alive in RAT POO!"

NO!! We must
make them leave
RIGHT NOW!

Granny Goat
shrieked.

Everyone

TUMBL

downstairs and
fell at the bottom,
all in a heap.

They paused in front of the
rats' door. No one wanted
to be the first to knock.

. . . a small,

tidy,

friendly looking rat

smiled up at them.

"Hello! Are you our new
neighbours?" she asked.

Another small,

tidy rat

joined her.

"I'm Betram and this is Natasha.
Will you join us for some
home-made cake?

We've just unpacked the dishes and were
planning to invite you over. Do come in!"

They bumbled inside. Everyone felt embarrassed – except the bunnies, who were excited about CAKE.

"How wonderful to have such thoughtful, welcoming new neighbours living here!" said Natasha.

"Yes," said Bertram. "We thought you might worry when you heard that rats had moved in. We know that rats aren't everyone's idea of the perfect neighbours!"

GULP

"OH NO!" gasped
Lettuce through a
mouthful of carrot cake.
"That thought NEVER crossed our minds!"
All the animals nodded their heads and blushed.

After they snaffled up the last crumbs of cake, they HOPPED and TROTTED and TOTTERED and PADDED and CLATTERED back upstairs . . .

Jake burped.